Teddy -
Bishopstone Station's Bear

Author's Pen

Worthing Road, Horsham, West Sussex, RH12 1TD

Published by Author's Pen, Worthing Road, Horsham, West Sussex. RH12 1TD

©2022, Sandra Gordon

The author's moral rights have been asserted.

First published, 2022

British Library Cataloguing in Publication Data available

ISBN 978-1-8383436-4-4 paperback

ISBN 978-1-8383436-5-1 e-book

Printed by Ingram Spark.
Typesetting, cover design and illustrations by Simon Cottrell, Horsham, West Sussex

Author's Pen

This book is dedicated to the memory of
Guy Wright whose teddy inspired this story.

About the author

Sandra Gordon took an adult learning course in creative writing at the College of Richard Collyer in Horsham and has since written many short stories for adults. *Teddy – Bishopstone Station's Bear*, is her first longer story written for children. Her love of writing and interest in trains – her grandfather was Stationmaster at Goldsborough Station near Harrogate – made writing this book a natural partnership.

She lives in Norfolk with her husband.

The proceeds from the sale of this book are to be shared jointly between Friends of Bishopstone Station (FOBS), and Cancer Research. You can find out more about the work to restore Bishopstone Station and how to visit the station on the FOBS website: F.O.B.S @fobs_seaford

Contents

Introduction

So often a teddy is given as the first gift to a new-born baby. It is a treasured possession with lots of precious memories and is often the toy kept as a sentimental reminder of childhood.

When this teddy was found at Bishopstone Station by members of Friends of Bishopstone Station (FOBS), I saw him in a photo and it gave me the inspiration for writing his story and for the fictional adventures he had with Ian.

In real life, Bishopstone Station's bear was owned by Guy Wright who – when he saw the article on local television – immediately recognised his teddy and contacted Barbara Smith, of FOBS, to claim him and other items from his childhood.

Although my story is fiction, I'm sure in real life Guy had lots of fun and adventures with his teddy.

Guy's teddy is now finally back home where he belongs. Sadly, Guy died not long after being reunited with his teddy but his family were delighted with my story and have given it their blessing.

Chapter  1

Bishopstone Station

For the last forty years, Teddy has listened to the rumble of trains passing through Bishopstone Station. He has lain in a rickety wooden box on a cold concrete floor, inside a gloomy room at the side of the station. Alongside him are a couple of well-thumbed books, scraps of paper, chipped metal cars, a pen-knife and a small bag of marbles.

Today, after so long in the blackness of the box, Teddy hears a noise. Muffled voices. What is happening? His eyes widen in anticipation. Can this finally be the day? Is his wait over? The roller shutter clatters and rattles into life and shoots up with a crash. He hears a jumble of objects spill onto the hard floor.

Teddy's box is at the back of the room amongst old car parts, some wooden oars and a skateboard. He hears eager voices – none are ones he recognises.

'At last! Hurrah, we've finally got into the parcel office.'

Teddy hears clapping, loud excited voices and the sound of people walking about the room. 'Goodness, I can't believe how much stuff is in here. Look at that pair of wooden skis and there's an oar … and a fishing rod.'

Another voice, trembling with excitement, 'Moira, look — Look, there's some tattered station signs—Oh, and look, … these photos bring back memories!'

Through a gap in the box, Teddy sees a man step back and sigh wistfully; the man is staring at some old railway posters.

Teddy hears the rustle and crunch of boxes being shoved and opened and the rise and fall of shrill voices as more items are discovered and examined. Then he hears someone fumbling to open the box he's lying in, alongside the cherished items that were once so important to their owner. His eyes widen and his little body tenses, not daring to believe his wait could finally be over.

'Oh, look in this box—It's full of kid's toys including a cute – if slightly grubby, teddy bear.'

Teddy looks hopefully into the face of the stranger who picks him up, pokes his tummy, then places him on top of the other boxes. The stranger is not Ian. He tries to remember the room where he was left all those years ago, but he is confused. Where have all the sweet jars gone? The shelves full of lemon sherbets, toffees, humbugs, Dolly Mixtures and all the other brightly coloured sweets in the station shop where so many children would eagerly come and spend their pocket money? Where is the counter and the big cash register that always gave that ka-ching sound before coins were thrust into the cash drawer? Oh, and the lovely sickly, sweet smell that lingered in the little shop – gone and replaced with the strange, pungent smell of murky, oily car parts.

An image comes to him and he remembers the day he fell from Ian's pocket onto the sweet shop floor, where Mary had rescued him. Then another image, so much later when he had been put in a box and stored in Father's workshop – long forgotten by the boy who had once owned him.

Teddy blinks a few times but the picture doesn't change. His golden bead eyes mist over as he thinks long and hard. Slowly, very slowly, he tries to make sense of his scrambled memories from the last forty-years and struggles to remember …

Chapter  2

Christmas 1976

The snow falls late in the afternoon on Christmas Eve. Ian and Robert – wrapped snug in their coats – dash outside and spin in the middle of the garden.

Everything is soon coated in a blanket of snow. The two boys are shouting, playing aeroplanes; their arms outstretched. Icy flakes land on their faces and vanish in an instant. There is just time for a snowball fight before teatime. They come inside wet and soggy, boots squelching on the kitchen floor.

'Mind you don't make a mess before your

father comes home; otherwise, you'll be for it!' says Mam.

Amidst laughter, Ian and Robert squabble for the towel as they dry their hands. Ian squats down and rubs the towel over the scattered drops of snow from their coats.

'Ian! Don't use the towel as a floor cloth! Get one out of the cupboard,' chides his mam. Hands on hips, she shakes her head at the sight of the dirty towel.

Robert laughs and pulls a face and Ian sticks out his tongue in response, then trudges to find the cloth. Ian is too happy to care, because tomorrow will be Christmas Day and he cannot wait for that magical time, when he and his brother will wake early and open stockings bulging with presents.

***

After tea they sit in front of the fire and watch as their notes to Father Christmas, blaze and burn in the hot embers.

'But how will Father Christmas know what we want, when all the paper has burnt and there's nothing left to read?' Ian's eyes narrow and a frown creases his forehead as he looks across at his father, waiting for an answer.

Sat in the wooden rocking chair, pipe balanced on his chest, Father grunts then leans forward, 'See all the paper going up the chimney? When it gets to the top, it flies off to Greenland and one of those elves will catch the bits, stick them together and hand them to Father Christmas. That's how he'll know.'

Ian is not convinced. The creases on his forehead remain but he dare not question his father, fearful his presents will not appear. He likes the magic of Christmas and the thought of Father Christmas coming down their old brick chimney with his sack full of toys, even if he is not so sure about this note business.

Robert sighs and Ian looks up at his brother.

'Let's hope the elf can read our writing and

doesn't get our presents muddled up—I don't want a teddy bear!'

But Ian does. He knows that most of his friends have asked for microscopes and footballs this year. He knows he is two years older than Robert and that Robert has already outgrown his bear. But ever since Ian's first teddy was left behind on a beach while they were on holiday, he had wanted something to hug and cuddle when he has laid awake at night and watched the strange patterns swirling on the bedroom ceiling from the streetlights. He wants something to hold when his dreams come alive, wake him, make him sit up with a jump.

A teddy will protect him from the wizards and witches who, in past dreams have chased him. Will protect him from the trees in the forest whose branches have turned to arms and tried to entangle him. Protect him from the black crow who swoops down trying to peck off his ear. Ian knows a teddy will soon sort them all out.

'There'll be no presents for either of you

boys, if you don't get off to bed,' says Father, getting out of his seat as the boys rush past him, up the stairs to their rooms.

**

Christmas morning and the boys wake early, run downstairs to the sitting room and head for the piles of brightly wrapped presents. With lots of shouting and squealing, the paper is soon strewn over the floor.

Robert pushes his dark blue shiny racing-car along the track making vroom-vroom noises before carefully parking it in its plastic garage. Ian makes pictures with his Etch A Sketch, twists and turns the knobs, shakes the screen and starts again.

There are lots of smiles and laughter as their parents look on and every so often Ian gazes across at his presents, guarded by his favourite – a teddy. At last! And what a smart looking teddy he is. Cherry red fur for his ears and body, while his head and arms are a buttery yellow. A tweaked little nose above the stitched line for his mouth, and golden bead shaped eyes – not smiling but with a knowing look that says, *I'm your friend and I belong to you.* Ian smiles back at him. He knows tonight he will sleep soundly and safely with Teddy by his side.

There is a knock at the door, more laughter and on a wave of high spirits his cousins, auntie and uncle, granny and gramps bowl into the house, wishing them a happy Christmas. Ian and Robert jump up and down; thrilled to see their cousins, Gary and Marie, and to show off their presents. They duck and dive away from being kissed by Granny.

Then the four cousins sit on the floor, near the Christmas tree, to play with their new toys. Auntie Sheila and Granny – arms laden with food – wander into the kitchen as the mouth-watering smell of almost cooked turkey wafts around the house.

Uncle Stan and Gramps stand in the narrow hall, backs pressed against the wall as Father hands each of them a glass of beer. He pours a

Martini for Mam and Auntie Sheila and mixes a Snowball for Granny; they raise their glasses to a very happy Christmas!

Chapter 3

Visiting Father in his Workshop

In the last couple of days, the snow has melted and turned to rain. Ian and Robert stare out of the window. They had lots of fun playing with their new toys, but today they had wanted to meet up with their friends and build a snowman.

'Maybe it will snow again tomorrow?' says Robert, sliding from his seat onto the floor to start parking his toy cars.

Ian is not so sure, 'Mam, can we go and see Father at the workshop?'

'If you must, but don't forget to put your

coats on,' says his mam from the kitchen.

Robert and Ian are already out of the door and racing down the street. Heads down against the rain and buttoning their coats as they run. They head from the cul-de-sac towards the railway station, where their father catches the train to London for his job as a mechanic at the Houses of Parliament.

On one side of the main entrance is a workshop – which their father rents. It is full of car parts. Tins of oil and paint and twisted pieces of metal which both boys are always reminded to be careful not to knock into as they wander round watching their father drilling, sawing, painting and making good what is broken.

Their father loves working at Bishopstone Station and he has often told them how unusual it is to find an eight-sided building. When he had first got the workshop there, he had sat them – one on each knee – and told them that it had been built in 1936 in the Art deco style which had given it a modern and stylish look with sleek lines and shapes. They have heard this story so many times since then that they can repeat it word for word.

On the opposite side of the main ticket kiosk, there is a small shop – a sweet shop. It is the real attraction, where most of the local kids' pocket money is spent. Jars full of different coloured sweets, all lined up with funny names like Blue Bird Toffees, gob-stoppers, Black Jacks, aniseed twists. All waiting to be bought and eaten.

From his coat pocket, Ian takes out some money he has been given by Granny for Christmas. Hidden in his inside pocket is Teddy, who has been bounced and shaken as the boys ran down the street. Robert peers eagerly over his brother's shoulder.

'Cor, you've got some money. What shall we buy?'

Ian scowls at his younger brother, knowing full well he will have to share his bag of sweets, otherwise Robert will tell their mam – or worse their father!

'Okay,' says Ian. 'Let's go and see Mary before we visit Father,' they both do an about-turn and head for the sweet shop.

***

The bell attached high on the door of the sweet shop makes its usual clinking noise as Ian pushes it open.

'Yes m'ducks, what would you like?' says Mary, her round friendly face smiles down at the boys from behind the counter as she watches Ian scan the jars trying to decide.

'Mmm, I think I'll have a quarter of fruit pastilles, please,' says Ian. Mary turns to take down the glass jar, unscrews the shiny, silver lid and carefully shakes out the sugar-coated sweets. Ian watches them tumble onto the scales.

Mam often reminds them that they have known Mary since they were born. While their mam works, their father, Jack, has occasionally brought them to his workshop and looked after them in the back – out of the way of his tools.

Mary often tells them they are lovely little boys. As far as they are concerned, they are just like most kids in their street and enjoy coming to buy sweets and seeing their mates before heading to the park. Secretly though, Ian loves to see her and he thinks Robert does too.

'Didn't expect you two in the shop today. Thought you'd be home playing with all your new toys?'

Ian nods, busy chewing the lime pastille, sweet and sour collide and tingle on his tongue. Robert jumps up and down, tries hard to reach into the brown paper bag that Ian holds aloft.

'We wanted to build a snowman but the rain has washed away the snow, so we came to see Father instead,' says Ian. He reaches into his sweet bag and hands Robert a pastille.

'Well, mind you say hello to your father

before you go home,' Mary winks at Ian. He realises that she knows full well the real reason why they have come to the station.

Ian smiles at her, shoves the bag into his pocket, finishes his pastille and pushes Robert ahead of him as he walks out of the shop and over to see his father.

***

The familiar smell of oil and petrol meets them as the boys push open the door into the workshop. Father is clad in dark green overalls, glasses perched on top of his head. He nods to them and continues to file a piece of metal held firmly in the jaws of a bench clamp.

'What's that?' asks Robert pointing at the metal.

'That is a brake drum and it's what makes a car stop,' says their father. 'When you're older you'll be able to learn all about cars and how they work,' The boys peer under an open bonnet, trying to fathom out the engine.

Their father takes the time to explain what he is doing. Ian always enjoys these chats, his father seems happiest when he is doing his job and describing it to him and his brother.

At the piercing sound of drilling on metal, Robert puts his hands over his ears and runs outside. Ian follows to escape the noise. As they stand together, Mary appears, pulls her arm from behind her back, and there, clasped in her large, bony hand is, Teddy!

***

After she's gone, Robert rounds on Ian, 'You brought Teddy? I can't believe you brought him along!' he dances and jumps round Ian making baby noises.

Ian, scarlet-faced and angry, grabs Robert and pushes him against the shop window but Robert trips and falls onto the pavement. Above Robert's wails, Ian hears the bell's clink as the sweet shop door opens.

'Hey, steady on boys, it's only a bear,'

Mary's thick arms separate them as they writhe and wriggle out of her grasp. Robert breaks free first, turns and runs towards home.

As Ian waves goodbye to Mary and chases after Robert, he feels the comforting shape of Teddy back in his inside pocket. He must have fallen out while he was busy buying sweets. Ian feels silly. He had never meant to bring Teddy and had forgotten he was in his pocket. If only they had been able to build their snowman, he had intended to sit Teddy on top.

Chapter 4

Where's Teddy?

Teddy sits high on a shelf in Ian's bedroom. He's been tossed behind the big globe of the world that spins satisfyingly whenever it is turned. From his usual position on Ian's bed, Teddy has watched it whirl many times till his head has felt dizzy and his body woozy – ready to crumple in a heap on the floor. But today, the globe is still and its shiny hard surface hides him. From one golden eye, he can see bits of the room, Ian's unmade bed, books cluttering the floor, Action Man wrestling with some unknown soldier and the ears of the bouncy Space Hopper peeping out from the cupboard.

Teddy's still not sure why Robert threw him onto this high shelf. After breakfast Robert had tip-toed into Ian's room, grabbed Teddy, climbed on the chair and roughly hurled him onto this shelf.

At first it had been fun to look down and watch everything, but now Teddy is cold and the shelf is hard. He wants to be back in Ian's soft, comfy bed, sleepily dreaming and waiting for his boy to come home. But no one's found him. Instead, he can hear the drone of the vacuum cleaner, voices calling, doors closing and opening, music on the wireless and sounds from a car parked outside.

The day drifts by and turns to early evening. The room darkens, the sun dips out of view and the shadows cast by the streetlights leave jagged lines over Ian's bed. Teddy hears the boys come home from school. Dishes clatter as tea is served. Father's gruff voice greets them. Silence as the family eats, followed by the playful voices of the boys enjoying the last minutes of the day before bath time and bed.

***

Teddy watches as Ian wanders into his bedroom. Mam is right behind.

'Oh, Ian you've not made your bed – what a mess. Here, come and help before your bath.' Ian pulls a face and reluctantly drags at the bed covers and makes a feeble attempt to help his mam.

Both boys head for the bathroom and Teddy can hear them splashing and spluttering in the bath and laughing and shouting as Mam forever tells them to *hurry up*.

Ian drags the towel behind him into the bedroom, tugs on his pyjamas, lays on his bed and flicks through a comic.

'Five minutes, then lights out,' says Mam. She picks up the towel and kisses Ian on the top of his head.

Teddy hears her light tread on the stairs. Head still in his comic, Ian climbs under his covers. Teddy watches as Ian stops and pulls back the covers, looks under the bed, round the room. As he sees the panic appear on Ian's face, Teddy holds his breath. Ian has realised – Teddy is missing.

'I'm up here,' Teddy wants to shout. But he can't. He can only watch as Ian searches through the cupboards and finally shouts.

'Mam … I can't find Teddy. Have you seen him?'

There is a brief pause before Teddy hears Mam shout back. Her footsteps are heavy as she walks back upstairs.

She appears in Ian's doorway, 'Where did you last have him?'

'In bed … I left him in bed this morning, Mam. He's just disappeared. I can't see him anywhere.' Teddy can hear trembling in Ian's voice.

'Alright, alright, calm down. We'll find him.'

Teddy hears Robert's sniggers, followed shortly after by the rhythmic sound of his snores.

Meanwhile, Ian and Mam keep searching. Cupboards are emptied, clothes heaved out of drawers, the mattress rolled onto its side. Ian's father shouts from downstairs, telling Ian to get to bed. Ian looks at Mam, his eyes wild with desperation. Teddy knows it is pointless and they cannot see him. For the first time since Christmas Day, Ian will be going to bed alone – without him.

Ian and Teddy spend an uncomfortable, restless night. Around midnight, Ian thrashes in his bed, then sits bolt upright. Mam has to come and hug him back to sleep and Teddy watches, upset at being unable to keep Ian safe from one of his troublesome dreams.

The following morning, Ian sits on the edge of his bed. He is directly opposite the shelf where Teddy has spent the night, 'Oh, Teddy, where have you gone?'

Unbeknown to Ian, Teddy has a plan. He blinks a few times, concentrates hard and tries to remember that giddy, light-headed feeling he had got from watching the globe whizz round. Absorbed by the effect, he feels woozy and a little shaky; his body knocks the globe. The movement is miniscule, but enough for Ian to notice the slight twitch of the globe. He looks at the shelf, squints, then climbs onto a chair, stretches out his arm and, wiggling his fingers he finally grasps Teddy.

'Teddy!' Ian shouts and hugs Teddy's red and yellow body tightly, then races downstairs to tell Mam.

Chapter 5

The invitation

There is a loud ding-dong of the bell. Ian wanders over and opens the front door to find the postman who hands him a large, white envelope addressed in spidery writing to his father. In the corner he sees a strange symbol.

Mooching into the kitchen, he puts the envelope on the table and sighs as he looks at his homework. It is Saturday morning and he should be out playing, but Mam has made him stay in to finish his school project on the planets. He cannot wait for May half-term and a week away from school and his annoying teachers!

'Who was at the door?' asks Mam; she stands at the sink washing the breakfast dishes.

'Postman. Letter for Father. A fancy one,' Ian hands her the envelope.

She stares at the symbol and reads, 'Houses of Parliament.' then runs her fingers over the strange symbol he has wondered at. 'Goodness,' she says. 'this looks important. I think we'd better put it somewhere safe until your father gets home, so he can open it.'

Ian turns to the pages of the bulky encyclopaedia, continues his drawing and then begins writing sentences about Jupiter, Saturn and Venus until he has exhausted the useful facts his teacher will find interesting.

***

He runs upstairs to his bedroom, pulls on a jumper, takes a quick look under the covers to make sure Teddy is still there, then heads out of the door. Ever since Teddy mysteriously disappeared all those months before, Ian has taken great care to check he is always tucked under the covers in his bed. He feels sure Robert was somehow involved in Teddy's disappearance but he has never been able to prove it.

***

Outside the boys play in the garden. Lots of shouting; kicking the ball constantly against the wall. Thud, thud, thud.

'Kick it to me,' yells Robert to his brother. 'I'm in goal.'

Ian drags the dustbin in front of the garage wall and hauls an empty flowerpot over to make another goalpost.

Robert's loud scream interrupts the thud, thud, thud of the ball, followed by his noisy crying and shouts for Mam. She rushes outside to see what all the commotion is about.

'Oh Ian,' Mam yells. 'How could you have kicked the ball so hard. Look at your brother's nose!' She pinches Robert's nose and tips his head back before putting his fingers in place of her own and rushing back inside for a cold, wet towel.

Dejected, Ian sits by the side of the bin until Mam returns.

'Mam, I … I … I'm sorry. I didn't mean to kick the ball in Robert's face. He's the goalie. It was an accident.'

'Yes, you did! You did it on purpose … you did … you did,' wails Robert, spitting blood. Ian watches Mam wrap the towel turban-style round Robert's head. Robert's face is smeared with blood, eyes red from crying as he shouts about how much it hurts.

Head in his hands, Ian keeps repeating *he's sorry* as Robert's blood congeals and he quietens, sitting on the back doorstep next to Ian and holding a flap of the towel to his nose. He is quietly impressed with the strength of his kick. Mam looks him over.

'Never mind … never mind, these things happen,' she gives Ian a gentle cuff across the head as she walks between the boys and back inside. With one hand on the door jamb, she turns, 'Now, behave yourselves until your father gets home. And Robert, sit still for a few more minutes till the bleeding has completely stopped.'

***

Jack clears away his tools and tidies up his station workshop. It has been a productive morning and he has managed to fix the swivel wing-mirror and rubbed down the front wing ready for respraying. The Vauxhall Viva will look as good as new.

He smiles to himself. It always amuses him whenever he is asked where he works and he happily says, 'The Houses of Parliament.' It doesn't matter that it is the mechanics' garage beneath the Houses of Parliament, by then the look on the face of the person who has asked says it all! *'Impressive or what,'* Jack says to himself.

Having a second workshop at the station allows him to store and source various parts for cars that he can't always get in the City. And the City prices! Those dealer boys in the trade know how to charge, especially for Members of Parliament! Whereas when he asks around locally, he can pick parts up for a lot less money; getting a good deal for him and his employers.

Jack glances at his watch. Time for lunch and an afternoon at home with his feet up watching the footie on the TV. Hopefully he can avoid having to play football in the garden with the boys!

***

'Letter for you love,' Carol hands Jack the large white envelope as he walks into the kitchen.

He whistles when he sees the Houses of Parliament portcullis symbol and tears open the envelope.

'I hope you haven't got the sack,' Carol says, her tone flippant.

'No way; not the sack,' Jack's voice rises in excitement. 'Just an invite to the annual tea party for staff and their families!' he waves the invitation enthusiastically in front of her face. 'How about that?! Little old garage mechanic and his family mixing with the toffs of the Labour Government.'

'When is it? When is it?' asks Carol excitedly, standing on tiptoe to read the invitation.

'Saturday, 26th June. Perfect. There was a rumour they were going to invite the lads from the garage this year. Those of us that do a hard day's graft!' Jack laughs as he whisks Carol into a bear hug and whispers in her ear. 'Better get yourself a new dress, gal. Gotta look your best! And make sure those two young ruffians outside scrub up good.' Jack looks out of the kitchen window and smiles as he watches Ian and Robert running round the garden, chasing after the football. It looks as if he will get a quiet afternoon with the football after all.

At lunch, Jack sits between his sons and shows them the invite. He explains that they have been invited to a party in London where he works. The boys listen, suitably excited and wide-eyed. Robert asks what the Houses of Parliament are.

***

That night in bed, Ian explains to Teddy about the invite and how he intends to bring Teddy with him, so they can see London together.

Chapter  6

School assembly

Ian and Robert stand side by side on the wooden stage; unsure where to look or what to do. Out of the corner of his eye, Ian watches Robert *fiddle* – as Mam would say – with his buttons. Ian nudges his brother with his elbow to make him stop. Their head-teacher, Mrs Williams, talks about him and Robert.

'So, boys and girls, Ian and Robert have been invited to a party at the Houses of Parliament with their parents—How exciting is that! Now, who knows where the Houses of Parliament are? … Anyone?' she asks.

Silence in the room until a boy sticks up his hand and shouts, 'London, Miss.'

'Well done, Brian. And who do you think Ian and Robert are hoping to meet at this party? Who is the person in charge of the Government that makes all the rules? Does anyone have any ideas?' Mrs Williams looks round the room at blank faces.

'The Queen?' a lone voice shouts from the back.

'No, no, not The Queen,' she says shaking her head at the laughter that's sprung up around the room. 'It's a gentleman called, Mr James Callaghan. He's the Prime Minister, boys and girls, and he has lots of people helping him run the country. They are called Members of Parliament or MP's and they all sit in the House of Commons and discuss how to run the country.' She turns towards where Ian stands, nervously twisting the edge of his sweater. 'We're all looking forward to hearing about your exciting trip to London, Ian and Robert. Will you tell us all about it in assembly next week?'

Ian's eyes widen at the very thought of having to stand up in assembly and talk. As the eldest, he has no doubt it will have to be him. He feels the anxiety build in his stomach. He gulps a few times, trying not to think about it.

Chapter  7

Houses of Parliament

Jack stands in the hallway and looks at his family. A big smile appears on his face. Carol twirls in her new dress. The boys are looking smart, standing to attention in their shirts and ties and the checked jackets that one of Carol's friends has rustled up on her Singer sewing machine. His family have done him proud! He beams with pride and looks forward to showing them off to his colleagues and the *toffs* at the Houses of Parliament.

As they march out of the door, turning towards Bishopstone Station to catch the train to London, Carol repeats the strict orders she's given the boys, *walk nicely, no messing about and NO fighting!*

Jack is not exactly sure who they will be meeting. He knows quite a few people who will be going. Anyway, it is his mates he is looking forward to seeing and having a bit of a laugh and a giggle with … as well as something to eat and drink. He pats his pocket for the umpteenth time, checking he has got the four invitations to get them through security and into the Houses of Parliament.

***

Ian and Robert sit side by side on the train. Green fields and trees whizz past. A uniformed man sells drinks but Mam will not let them have one, in case they spill it down their new clothes. Robert moans and begins to cough, so Father gives in and asks the man for a glass of water.

Ian just manages to wrestle the glass for a sip but he is careful not to wriggle around too much because – unbeknown to his family – hiding in the lining of his jacket is – Teddy!

Secretly hidden and brought along to be part of the family outing.

The train journey seems to take forever. *When will we be there?* - the boys ask every few minutes. Eventually the fields disappear, the colours and shapes change. Rows of houses appear, back gardens, then grubby sky-scrapers reach high into the clouds with washing strung across their balconies, waving in the wind. Ian and Robert's noses are pressed to the window. Father points out Battersea Power Station, its four chimneys blackened, tall and imposing. The boys twist and turn in their seats and try to see to the very top where steam trails across the blue sky. Then the train begins to slow, its wheels grind and grate on the tracks as it edges into Victoria Station.

Ian and Robert hold hands and hurry to keep up, following their parents through the station. Outside, they wait as a double decker bus lumbers to their stop. They scramble up the stairs; racing to get to the best seats at the front. From the window they see bikes swerving to avoid people crossing the road, cars tooting their horns and almost touching as the queue of traffic stretches ahead.

Tall buildings on either side engulf the bus. Ian would love to bring Teddy out and hold him up to the window but he knows if Robert sees him, he will only *tell on him* so he bides his time.

They arrive at the Cromwell Green entrance to the Houses of Parliament and their invites are checked by a hefty looking security man. Then they are escorted towards the central lobby of the Houses of Parliament. The boys stand, mouths open, straining their necks to see the magnificent carved walls towering above them to dizzying heights; soaring arches surround stained glass leaded windows, huge mosaics are decorated with the patron saints of the countries of the United Kingdom. They tiptoe on the tiled floor and circle round and round taking everything in. Ian puts his hand over his jacket, he can feel his heart pounding through the material.

'Look boys,' says Father. 'that's Sir Winston Churchill. He helped Britain win the Second World War.' They stand solemnly in front of the statue; a sudden, loud, booming voice makes them jump.

'Fancy meeting you here, Jack,' it is Joe, one of Father's workmates.

'Didn't recognise you in all that fancy gear,' jokes their father. He and Joe stand together grinning mutely before Jack turns to introduce Joe to Carol and the boys.

More people arrive, Ian watches his father calling out different names, shaking hands, chatting and laughing. It is all very jolly until a man appears with a loud gong that echoes and vibrates around the lobby. The gong makes Ian's ears ring.

'Ladies and gentlemen, boys and girls, this way please to the Terrace Dining Rooms where a buffet will be served.'

Robert looks at Ian, 'What's a buffet?' he whispers to his brother. Ian shrugs, pulls a face; he doesn't know either but he is not letting on. As they fall into line with the stream of people whose voices have risen to an excited babble of laughter and shouted hellos, he and Robert shuffle along in front of their parents. Ian remembers what Mam has told them and keeps his hands out of his pockets.

It is quite a gathering and the crowd spreads out, finds seats. They listen to instructions from the waiters rushing about with trays of food. What a bun-fight! Well, an orderly bun-fight is how Mam describes it to the boys. They sit along one wall of the dining room. She appears through the throng of people and sits next to them on a long row of chairs, two plates of food carefully balanced on her right arm and another in her left hand.

'Where's your father?' she asks them and Ian can hear the annoyance in her voice and knows it is because their father is probably chatting somewhere with his mates.

She pushes the plates of food at them, telling them to, eat up. Ian looks at the food. He recognises the ham and bread, small round potatoes and bits of lettuce, but there's other food, stuff he has never seen, 'What's this Mam?' he asks pointing to a round of pastry.

'Vol au vents – bits of pastry filled with chicken – try them.'

Ian takes a mouthful. The chicken's gooey sauce squelches into his mouth, a bit dribbles down his chin. It is the most delicious thing he has ever tasted.

'Mam, please can I go and get another?' Mam nods and Ian dashes off.

As he jostles through the crowd, he notices other boys and girls all smartly dressed like him and Robert. Some of the women are wearing impossibly large hats and the men are in a variety of suits, some of them badly fitting, but all are talking, laughing and cracking jokes while trying to balance plates of food and drinks.

By the time Ian reaches the large rectangular table there is little left. He looks round – miffed that the mouth-watering pastries have disappeared. One of the waiters appears next to him.

'What are you after, young man,' the waiter smiles at him and stacks the empty plates.

Ian looks at him, his eyes squint as he tries to remember what Mam had called the delicious chicken pastry.

'A volley-vont,' he says looking at the waiter hopefully.

The waiter lets out a small laugh, 'Follow me to the kitchens and let's see if we can find you a *volley-vont*,' he laughs again kindly.

Ian ducks and dives to keep up with the waiter who marches through with his pile of plates. They walk out of the room and into a maze of corridors. In the distance, Ian hears the hum of people working. Orders are shouted, metal clangs, plates clatter onto work surfaces.

He has never been inside a kitchen as huge as this one. Or seen so many people wearing white aprons, expertly serving out so much interesting and appetising looking food.

'Any vol-au-vents left?' shouts the waiter Ian has somehow managed to keep up with. 'The young lad here has taken a fancy to them – mind you, he thinks they're *volley-vonts!*'

There's a ripple of laughter among the chefs and other waiters. One of the chefs walks over to Ian, 'What's your name lad?'

'Ian,' he replies, his voice barely above a whisper.

The chef wraps the pastry mounds in a thick white cotton napkin, taking care not to squish the oozing filling. He presents them to Ian, a faint aroma of chicken wafts from the folds of the napkin, 'There you are Ian. You enjoy them.'

'Cor, thanks mister,' Ian says, beaming from ear to ear.

With that, the waiter Ian had originally followed reappears and retraces his fast-paced steps. Ian dashes after him. Without his arms full of plates, the waiter moves too quickly for Ian who is cradling his food parcel and trying not to squash its contents.

He can just about see the waiter at the end of a long, darkly lit corridor ahead and then he vanishes. Ian panics and speeds up – did we come right or left, he thinks, taking the right-hand corridor. His heart beats rapidly. The corridor ahead ends with a door and – clinging tightly to Teddy around the volley-vents – Ian cautiously opens it.

Abrupt sunlight streaming through the tall, leaded window makes him blink. There's no sign of the waiter and Ian suddenly feels very tired. The green velvet chairs look so inviting. He sits down, opens up the food parcel and puts Teddy on the seat next to him. They are two interlopers momentarily unaware of their plush, extravagant surroundings.

Ian munches his chicken and pastry and gazes round at the intricate wood panelling, ornately carved fireplace and huge chandeliers hanging majestically from the ceiling as the sunlight dances through the glass. In between mouthfuls he explains to Teddy about the waiter, the kitchen, the wonderful food and getting lost. Ian licks his fingers, leans back in the chair and with Teddy balanced on his full tummy, he sighs contentedly and falls fast asleep.

Chapter 8

Ian gets lost

'Calm down, calm down, we'll find him. Don't worry.' Jack has his arm around Carol, trying to comfort her. She lets out little sobs while his friends and their families stand around with anxious faces.

They have both searched the dining room and there's no sign of Ian. A sense of panic descends with the realisation that he is missing. A couple of people remember seeing him at the food table. Then someone remembers seeing him walk out of the room. The man who banged the gong issues orders to the waiters to organise a search party. One of them pushes to the front, explaining that a young lad had followed him to the kitchen.

'I got him some vol-au-vents and then I thought he was following me back here,' the young waiter splutters the words and Jack can see his genuine concern and guilt.

'That'll be him. That'll be our Ian,' says Carol. She blows her nose in her cotton hankie and starts sobbing again.

'Right,' says the man who banged the gong, 'Let's head towards the kitchens.'

***

Unaware of all the commotion he is causing, Ian's sleep is disturbed by someone jiggling his arm. In the midst of his sleep, he can hear an anxious, insistent voice.

'Come along, young man. Wakey, wakey.'

Jolted awake, Ian opens his eyes with a start and lets out a short scream. The face that greets him is so close. Round and jolly, but it is the owner's eyebrows that startle Ian. He has never seen anyone with such enormous bushy eyebrows. Mouth wide open, he bolts upright; wondering where on earth he is. He grabs hold of Teddy, clutching him to his chest for protection.

'There, there young man, don't you worry. What's your name and what's your teddy's name? My name is Denis.'

'Ian, and he's my teddy. He's just called, Teddy.'

'Well, I am very pleased to meet you, Ian … and your Teddy – he's a very handsome looking bear. Do you know, when I was a little boy like you, I used to have a teddy just like yours. Took him everywhere with me. Even went fishing – until he fell in the river and got a bit wet.'

Ian smiles at this and relaxes a little. Denis asks if he came with his mother and father. Ian nods.

'I think they'll be extremely pleased to see you and I know exactly who you are now. You've caused quite a stir. Your parents thought you'd got lost in the corridors of the Houses of Parliament. We've been searching everywhere for you; when really all you wanted was a quiet snooze after your lunch.' He gives a little chuckle.

Ian smiles again, then the horror of what Denis has told him hits home, 'Oh no. Me mam and me father will kill me.'

'Now, now don't you worry. I'll explain how we've been having a nice little chat and that you got lost. Nothing to worry about. Come along, let's go and find your parents.' Denis holds out his hand and Ian jumps off the seat, holding Teddy in one hand and grabbing hold of Denis' outstretched hand with the other.

He can hear Denis talking, but he seems to be talking to himself, so Ian can only hear bits of what he's saying.

'Yes … just along here … I think we've got just enough time for me to give you a quick tour.'

Denis opens a door and Ian follows him into an enormous room filled with row after row of comfy looking green leather benches. He's never seen such a huge room or so many seats all ordered and straight, like a huge school assembly hall. Gigantic lights are suspended from the heavily beamed wooden ceiling.

'Now Ian, do you know what this room is called?'

Ian shakes his head. He holds Teddy in front of him as they circle the room.

Denis walks up to the front benches in the centre of the room, turns and proudly announces, 'This is the House of Commons, which is where the Prime Minister stands to address Members of Parliament,' he leans down conspiratorially, 'and you never know Ian, one day, I too might be Prime Minister.'

Suddenly, Ian realises how desperately he needs the loo, so he just nods his head in agreement. 'Please sir,' he announces solemnly. 'I need a wee!'

With one swift move, Denis escorts him from the chamber and hurries Ian through a wooden door that says WC in gold lettering. He points Ian to the men's lavatory – not a moment too soon!

Once they are back in the vast corridors, Ian hears lots of chattering and the clatter of people walking over stone floors. The sound stops Denis and Ian in their tracks; they wait to see who will appear.

Waiters, the man with the gong and a throng of other people march round the corner, heading straight for them.

Ian suddenly spots his mam, 'Mam, Mam!'

She runs headlong to him, shouting his name as she gathers him into her arms, laughing and crying at the same time, 'Oh Ian, where have you been? We've searched everywhere for you. You gave us such a fright.'

Between hugs, he explains how he couldn't keep up with the waiter who had given him the lovely chicken volley-vonts, but then he found a room where he fell asleep and then this nice man had found him and was giving him a tour.

'Indeed,' says Denis, 'we've had a lovely chat and a little walk through the House of Commons. I think both Ian and Teddy have had a jolly lovely time.'

'Oh no! You and that teddy – I didn't even know you'd brought it. You little rascal.'

Ian gives a shy smile as his father steps forward, apologising for all the fuss his son has caused.

'I'm really sorry, Mr Healey but thank you so much for finding him.'

'Not at all. Not at all. And remember Ian, you look after that teddy – I've still got mine in a cupboard somewhere at home. Awfully good to have a smart looking teddy like that!'

He winks at Teddy and much to Ian and Mr Healey's amazement, Teddy winks back!

Denis leans back down, his mouth close to Ian's ear, 'Goodness, did your Teddy just wink at me or am I seeing things?' Ian can't believe it either, he simply nods as Denis turns and walks down the corridor scratching his head.

The rest of the group look on grinning, unaware of the conversation Ian's just had with Denis Healey. They look amused.

'Fancy the Chancellor of the Exchequer admitting he still owns a teddy!' a woman says and they all laugh. Ian's not surprised at all. Mam gives Ian another hug.

Chapter  9

Parcel office, Bishopstone Station, 2021

Teddy's dreaming, but his happy memories are brought to a sudden halt. He is still in the parcel office, but now he has been moved and sits on top of a pile of boxes. It has been a few weeks since the Friends of Bishopstone Station first unlocked the roller shutters, and now there are people clambering around the room again. They talk, pick things up, spread them out and a lady with a clipboard keeps asking people to stand here, move there, hold the microphone, speak slowly.

Teddy is lifted into the air and the feeling brings back such memories of being held and cared for by Ian. His eyes widen and a surge of warmth spreads through him as he begins to remember.

'Okay, Moira, if you can hold the teddy in front of the wooden box where he was found … near the skis and oars and we'll start recording.' Teddy hears bits of the conversation.

'… found in the parcel office … been locked for over forty years … must belong to someone. A wooden box of memories including this much-loved teddy.'

Teddy stares ahead forlornly and wonders, *what's going to happen to me?*

***

It had been an eventful day of filming at Bishopstone Station in the once locked parcel room with its intriguing contents. Moira had been stood in front of the fascinating railway posters stuck to the walls, Teddy had listened to her answering questions from The Argus newspaper before she was interviewed on television by BBC South East Today.

Now, Moira puts Teddy back into his wooden box and buckles it into the front-seat of her car and they travel a short distance before she parks the car on a driveway in front of a house. Teddy wonders if this is his old home but it looks very different, even after forty years.

She stops the car and picks him out of the box, 'Well, Teddy, that was definitely an action-packed day and hopefully the filming will make more people aware of the restoration work we're doing at the station.' She drops her head wearily onto Teddy's. 'Oh dear!' she holds her nose and sneezes. 'You are a dusty bear.' Moira tucks him back in the box before she speaks again.

'I'll tell you what, Teddy; I never thought my involvement with the station would result in revealing so much intrigue and interest in a room that appears to have been used to store car parts. I still can't believe how much money we've raised!'

She rubs a thumb over the bedraggled stitching that is coming apart on his nose.

'You are a sweet, well-worn but sad looking bear. I hope someone out there will see you on television or in the paper and your little face will jog their memory.'

Teddy hopes so too and he thinks there is a real possibility that finally, after all the years apart he and Ian will be reunited.

Chapter 10

The reunion

A few days later, the local news report Moira had recorded about the railway station flashes onto her TV.

Teddy is sat on top of the wooden box, at the back of the room behind the sofa where Moira and her husband are watching the story. He can hear and see glimpses of himself on television. He listens, eyes wide and alert and he wonders and wishes for someone out there to remember him.

***

In a house nearby, Ian turns on the television and there staring at him from the screen is Teddy. His Teddy! His little face and bead eyes stare back at Ian – his worn-out cherry red and buttery yellow body – just as he had last seen him. He can hardly believe his eyes and sits in shock as the story unfolds about how Bishopstone Station's bear was found.

He remembers all those years ago when he and Teddy were inseparable and how he loved to share adventures with him. Most importantly, he remembers how he loved to talk with Teddy and share his fears and worries. Worries that, whenever Teddy was around, seemed to just melt away. With a pang, Ian remembers that as he grew older and more confident, Teddy hadn't been quite so important.

Oh, he had still snuggled up to him in bed, but when friends had come to stay for sleepovers it hadn't been *cool* to have Teddy in his bed. Regretfully, Teddy was either left on the floor or hidden behind a chair or shoved at the back of a drawer. Until, one day, Teddy had disappeared altogether.

Ian hadn't found out until years later that Mam had secreted Teddy and other items belonging to him and Robert in a wooden box. Eventually, the wooden box had been stored safely at his father's workshop at the station. When their father retired, he had kept the workshop for pottering around. But after Father had died nobody could find the key to the workshop.

In time Ian had forgotten about Teddy. As Ian sits and remembers, the news report continues to play out and says that Father's workshop was closed and everything from the station rooms was moved to the shuttered parcel office. Mothballed, forgotten, suspended in time to be covered in dust and wispy cobwebs.

Ian rings Robert as soon as the weather reports have finished, but Robert is only mildly interested; he had moved away many years ago and says, 'The toys we loved and treasured over the years wouldn't compete today with the likes of computer games, mobile phones and Xboxes.' Ian feels sad listening to Robert, but he is glad he has had the opportunity to play and have adventures. Not just with Teddy but with all the toys that were so important in his life.

It doesn't take him long to track down Moira and explain who he is and that Teddy and the other toys in the wooden box belong to him and his brother.

***

When Teddy hears the knock at Moira's door, he instinctively realises it will be Ian. There are voices in the hall and although he can't see Ian and the voice is deeper – he knows.

Teddy sits on the battered wooden box and when Ian walks into the room, a pang of nostalgia and sadness washes over Teddy. He swallows and blinks his scratched golden glass eyes to hide the emotion he feels at seeing Ian for the first time in forty years.

Ian picks him up, holds him, and looks straight into Teddy's golden eyes, and in Teddy's eyes he becomes the seven-year-old boy who shared his thoughts and secrets with Teddy and cuddled him tightly at night.

Teddy focusses on Ian's face and tries his hardest to smile at him, his little sewn lips stretch so wide. His eyes lock onto Ian's. Teddy remembers all their adventures and it is so good to be back with Ian – however different he looks!

A few weeks later a teddy restoration company called Nottingham Teddy Repairs, hears about the story and contacts Ian, offering to restore Teddy to his former glory.

In the time Teddy is away getting his fur replaced and his bright red and yellow body restored; his golden bead eyes cleaned and polished, his nose and body re-stuffed and the stitched smile extended across his face, Ian thinks about who would like to own Teddy. Robert is right; toys have changed so much since they were youngsters, but Ian feels sure any child will still love and want Teddy.

On Teddy's return, Ian sits down with his

youngest granddaughter, Ruby, and tells her his and Teddy's story. As Ian speaks, Ruby nods and stares solemnly into his eyes.

'What will you do, Grandad?'

From behind his back, Ian brings out Teddy and places him in Ruby's hands. She squeals with joy at the newly restored little bear, strokes his bright red and yellow furry body and looks into his shiny golden eyes and at the black stitched line under his re-tweaked nose. The one that gives him his sweet, crooked smile.

'Oh, Grandad, he's so handsome,' she hugs the bear close to her face. 'I'm going to love you forever, Teddy.'

And over her shoulder, as Ian looks on through misty eyes, Teddy winks at him.

Acknowledgements

Special thanks to Barbara Mine without whom the story of Teddy would not have happened had she not discovered, after decades of it being sealed, the old parcel room at Bishopstone Station where Teddy was found. And also, for her continued support, encouragement and input into the story.

A big thank you to Lesley Hart at Author's Pen for her patience, support, editorial suggestions and belief that the story would come to fruition.

I used the House of Commons website –
www.parliament.uk
and the Bishopstone Station websites to research my story:
https://railinsider.co.uk/2021/02/25/forgotten-artefacts-discovered-at-bishopstone-station/

Before you go...

Dear reader,

One last thing before you close Teddy's adventures ...

I hope you have enjoyed *Teddy – Bishopstone Station's Bear* and will add your review to Amazon, Goodreads and to your social media platforms. If you are happy to write a review for my book, then please share my book's cover with your social media review.

Thank you so much for reading Teddy's story and for supporting the Friends of Bishopstone Station and Cancer Research by purchasing this book.

Best wishes,

Sandra Gordon

UK Curriculum Spelling and Reading List Words

Teddy – Bishopstone Station's Bear includes lots of words from the UK curriculum spelling and reading lists to years three and four, which will help to develop your child's reading and spelling skills. The following words appear in the book:

accident	continue
actual	decide
address	describe(s)
answer	different
appear	disappear(ed)
arrive	early
believe	earth
breath	eight
build	enough
busy	extreme(ly)
business	favourite
centre	forward(s)
circle	fruit
complete(ly)	group

guard(ed)

heard

heart

height(s)

important

interest

learn

material

minute(s)

natural

notice

occasion(ally)

often

opposite

position

possess(ion)

potatoes

probably

purpose

quarter

question

remember

sentence(s)

separate

special

straight

strange

strength

though/although

thought

through

various

weight

woman/women

9 781838 343644